The subject matter and vocabulary have been selected with expert assistance, and the brief and simple text is printed in large, clear type.

Children's questions are anticipated and facts presented in a logical sequence. Where possible, the books show what happened in the past and what is relevant today.

Special artwork has been commissioned to set a standard rarely seen in books for this reading age and at this price.

Full-colour illustrations are on all 48 pages to give maximum impact and provide the extra enrichment that is the aim of all Ladybird Leaders.

A Ladybird Leader

lions
and tigers

written and illustrated by John Leigh-Pemberton

Ladybird Books Loughborough

Cats

Cats of every kind are alike
in many ways.

Lions, tigers and the other cats
in this book are all 'cousins'
of our pet cats.

Lions

Lions live in hot places.
Once they lived in
much colder parts of the world.
Perhaps that is why the male lion
has a mane.

The female lion is called a lioness.
She does not have a mane.

Lions — where they live
Nearly all the lions in the world
live in Africa.

There are a few left in India.

Once there were a great many there.

In Africa, lions live
on the huge, grassy plains.

They do not live in deserts,
or among mountains,
or in thickly wooded places.

Lions — how they live

Lions are hunters.
They kill and eat other animals.
When they are not hunting
they sleep for much of the time.

A pride of lions

Lions live in groups.
A fully-grown male lion
rules over several lionesses,
cubs and young lions.
This group is called a pride.

Lion cubs

Baby lions are called cubs.
From two to five are born
at the same time.
Their eyes are closed at birth.
They are quite helpless.

Lion cubs, like this month-old one,
are born with spotted fur.

Cubs open their eyes after a week.
After three weeks they can walk.
As they grow up,
they lose their spotted coats.

Cubs romp and play
for much of the time.
This helps to train them as hunters.

Lions — hunting

A pride of lions hunts as a team.

They usually hunt at night.

Sometimes they hunt by day.

The lionesses do most of the hunting.

Lions — feeding

In a year,
each lion kills about thirty animals.

Lions do not hunt every day.

Forty pounds (18.1 kg) of meat
makes a good meal for a lion.

Some of the animals hunted by lions

These are the lions' prey.

Blesbok,
an antelope

Thomson's
gazelle

Hartebees
a large
antelope

Zebra

Lions hunt mainly zebras, buffaloes, gazelles and antelopes.

There are many thousands of these on the plains where the lions live.

The African hunting dog

Leopards, cheetahs and hyenas
also live and hunt on the plains.

So do packs of African hunting dogs.

Even lions keep away from these dogs.

Lions — roaring

The area lived in by a pride of lions is called a territory.

The male lion usually roars to protect his pride and territory.

Only the 'big cats' roar.

These are the lion, tiger, leopard, snow leopard and jaguar.

Lions — teeth and tongue

Like all the cat family, lions use
their large teeth to tear their food.
They do not chew their food.
They swallow it in large lumps.

Their rough tongues help them
to swallow, and to clean
and smooth down their fur.

Cats' eyes

The eyes of lions, and of all
hunting animals, face forwards.

*In bright light the pupils of most cats' eyes
are narrow slits.
The pupil is the dark part in the centre
of the eye.*

*At night, or in dim light, the pupils
are large and round.*

All cats have good eyesight
by day and night.

Cats' feet

Cats have five toes on each front foot and four toes on each hind foot.

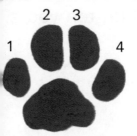

This is the mark of a lion's front paw. The extra toe (the same as our thumb) does not touch the ground, so leaves no mark.

Claws must be kept sharp for hunting and climbing. To protect them they are pulled back and hidden in sheaths when not needed.

A lion's front paw

extra toe

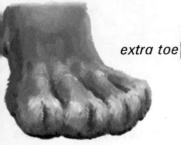

claws sheathed   claws ready for use

How long do lions live?

Lions are grown-up at about
four years old.
Only a few live longer than ten years.

Old lions live alone.
Lionesses usually stay with the pride
all their lives.

Lions in zoos

Zoo lions usually live longer
than wild ones.
They eat about ten pounds (4.5 kg)
of meat a day.

It is natural for a lion to hunt.
Zoo lions miss being able to hunt.

Tigers — where they live

Most of the wild tigers in the world live in the jungles of India.

A few live in China and in other parts of Asia.

Most tigers now live in hot countries.

Long ago they came from cold places like Manchuria and Siberia.

Tigers — how they live

Lions and tigers
are about the same size.

Their teeth, tongues, eyes and claws
are exactly alike.

Tigers do not live in groups,
as lions do.

They usually live alone.

Because tigers suffer from the heat,
they like to live in thick undergrowth.
Unlike lions, they spend much time
in water, getting cool.

Tigers are good swimmers.
They even catch and eat fish and frogs.

Tigers — hunting

Like lions, tigers hunt their prey
by stalking (creeping up on it).
When quite close, they spring on to it.
Lions hunt in groups. Tigers hunt alone.

*Chital or
spotted deer*

*Nilgai, a large
Indian antelope*

Sambar deer

Wild boar

These are some of the animals
which tigers hunt.

Why do tigers have stripes?

Stripes make the tiger difficult to see among reeds or tall grass.

This helps it to get near its prey, especially at night.

Tigers — feeding

Often tigers do not eat for a few days.
This is because they hunt alone
and food is hard to find.
Then they eat any food they can get.

When they get food, they feed
until they can eat no more.

Then they hide what is left.

Next day they return to it.

Man-eating tigers

Some tigers, like some lions and leopards, kill and eat men.

This usually happens when the animal is very hungry, old or wounded.

Tiger cubs

Three or four tiger cubs
are born at a time.
This is called a litter of cubs.

Tigers are fully grown at three years.
They can live for twenty years.
Usually they do not reach this age.

The tigers' voice

Tigers can roar,
as can all the 'big cats'.
They make many other noises,
such as a loud 'whoof'
and a sharp 'pook'.

The 'big cats' cannot purr
like a domestic cat.
All other cats can purr.

Northern tigers

A few still live in Manchuria and Siberia.

Very large, with long, pale fur and rather faint stripes.

Southern tigers

A very small number still live in Java and Sumatra.

Small, brightly coloured with short fur and very black stripes.

White tigers

In one part of India
there are some beautiful white tigers.
They have chocolate-coloured stripes
and blue eyes.

Tigers are rare

Every year there are fewer tigers.
They have been killed for 'sport'
and for their beautiful fur.

Animals which
tigers eat
are becoming scarcer.
Jungles, where tigers live,
are being cleared for farming.

The tiger might easily die out
as a wild animal.

If the tiger is to be saved,
men must stop hunting it.
We must not use its fur.
It must be allowed natural living space.

Leopards — where they live

Leopards live in many kinds of country,
where there are trees.

They live in jungles, forests,
grassy plains and among mountains.

There are leopards in India, China
and many other parts of Asia.

They are found also in most of Africa
and sometimes in Persia and Israel.

Leopards — hunting

Like lions and tigers,
leopards sometimes stalk their prey.
But often they lie in wait,
perhaps in a tree,
to catch a passing animal or bird.

Fireback pheasant

38

Leopards — climbing

Lions climb trees, but not often.
Tigers climb only when in danger.
Leopards spend much time
on the large branches of trees.
They often store food there
to protect it from hyenas.

Leopards' spots

Leopards are hard to see
in the leafy places where they live.
Their spotted fur looks like
a pattern of leaves and shadows.

Black leopards

Panther is another name for a leopard.
Some Indian leopards
which are nearly black,
are often called panthers.
Their dark spots can be seen
in sunlight.

Snow leopards

Snow leopards live among rocks
in the high, cold mountains of Asia.

Their long, pale-coloured fur
is hard to see against the rocks.

Clouded leopards

These small leopards live in the trees
of thick jungles in Asia.
The pattern of their fur is hard to see
among the trees.

Lynxes

Lynxes live in the cold parts
of America and Europe.
Their long fur keeps them warm.

Hares and birds are the main food
of lynxes and caracals.
Sometimes they kill larger animals.

The caracal

This is a kind of lynx which lives
in Africa and Asia in the hot deserts.
Because of the heat, it has short fur.

Lynxes and caracals have little tufts
of hair on the tips of their ears.
They have shorter tails than other cats.

Cheetahs

Cheetahs live on the grassy plains of Africa.

They hunt prey such as gazelle.

They first stalk their prey and then chase it over a short distance.

Cheetahs are the fastest runners
of all animals.

They can reach a speed of nearly
seventy miles (113 km) an hour.

Jaguars

The 'big cats' of South America
are the jaguars.
These powerful animals
live mostly in thick woodland.

The jaguar's pattern of spots
is different from the leopard's.

The jaguar has a dot in some rings
of his spots.

The leopard has no dot.

Jaguar's spot   *Leopard's spot*

Ocelots

The ocelot is a smaller cat
of South America.

This animal has been much hunted
for its beautiful fur.

Because it has been hunted so much,
it is now becoming quite rare.

So are many other spotted cats.

Pumas

Pumas are found in many parts
of North and South America.

Other names for the puma are — cougc
mountain lion, painter and catamount.

Pumas can live in all kinds of country.

Some live in deserts or mountains.

Others live in grassland or thick jungle

Wild cats

Wild cats live in several parts
of Europe.
Some live in Scotland.

Wild cats look very like tame cats.
They are about the same size.
Wild cats have longer legs,
thicker tails and bigger teeth.

Where the Cat Family lives

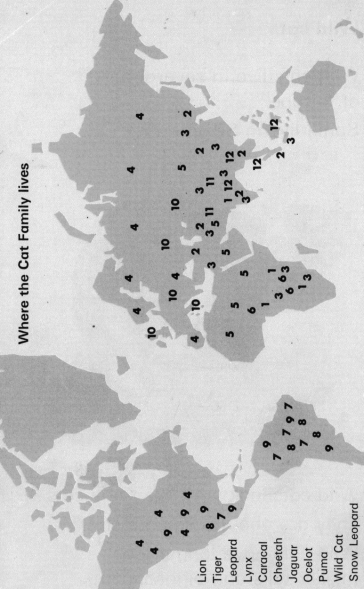

1 Lion
2 Tiger
3 Leopard
4 Lynx
5 Caracal
6 Cheetah
7 Jaguar
8 Ocelot
9 Puma
10 Wild Cat
11 Snow Leopard
12 Clouded Leopard